P9-DIA-717

ALSO BY CHARLTON HESTON

In the Arena

An Actor's Life

Beijing Diary

TO BE A MAN

Letters to My Grandson

CHARLTON HESTON

Simon & Schuster

SIMON & SCHUSTER
Rockefeller Center
1230 Avenue of the Americas
New York, NY 10020

Manufactured in the United States of America

10 9 8 7 6 5 4 3 2 1

Library of Congress Cataloging-in-Publication Data is available.
ISBN 0-684-84116-9

All photos by Lydia Heston unless otherwise indicated.

Frontispiece: Jack Alexander Clarke Heston (age 4) with his grandfather Charlton Heston on the set of the film Alaska *(directed by Jack's father, Fraser C. Heston.) October 1995.* Photograph courtesy of Castle Rock Films.

Acknowledgments

Michael Korda is the godfather of this book, to a far greater degree than is usually true of the head of a major publishing house. He thought of the idea for the book and, when I grumped at writing another one so soon ("I have a movie to do, Michael"), even gave me the title *To Be a Man: Letters to My Grandson.* Chuck Adams' editorial hand is as wise and patient as ever, the troops of able people at S&S also. We have a lot of wise and diligent people out here on our ridge, too, who among them keep me fed, in shape, and clothed. Running my work life, of course, is Carol Lanning, who pins notes to my jacket to get me to the right place every day. I thank them all, as well as my friends and colleagues. I thank you all, every one.

I offer this book, as I have my other books, to those at the center of my life, as indeed I offer them my work and my thanks for making it all possible. To Lydia, then; to Fraser and Marilyn, to Holly and Carlton and our new granddaughter Ridley . . . and of course to Jack, for whom the book was written, about the time we've spent together through all the days of his life. So far.

Jack Heston, age three months.

Foreword

While I was busy parting the Red Sea for Mr. DeMille, I was cast in the part of my life. I didn't have my usual leading man approvals, though . . . it was a package deal. We had no firm start date, an open-ended schedule and no set budget. I had some input on casting the star part, but Lydia and I had to share second billing. We were having a child.

Fraser Clarke Heston was fine in his role as a baby (you could say he was born for the part). When his sister, Holly, came along a few years later, our delights were doubled. Whoever said it first had it right: Your children are among the very best things in your life.

Five years ago, we were blessed again. Fraser and his wife, Marilyn, produced a boy child. Fray phoned at 3 A.M., the classic hour babies seem to choose to come into the world (why is this?). We raced through the predawn streets to the hospital, scooping up Marilyn's dad, Walter, en route, reenacting the scene we've all seen in a hundred movies.

Fray's birth had worked out a little differently. I was filming on location, some fifty miles from home. When I finished the day's shoot, I dozed in the back of the limo taking me to the studio, looking forward to a shower, then an evening at home with Lydia. Driving through the Universal Studios gate, we were stopped by the guard. "Mistuh Heston . . . I got a message from Production. "Yuh wife didn' want to distoib you onna set, but yuh should go straight to da' hospital. She's havin' yuh baby."

Good Lord! Now I'd not only be late for the first scene, I couldn't even remember the first lines! I froze, stone cold, then spotted a highway patrolman leaning on a big Harley, waiting for

Jack at sixteen weeks.

me. "Ahh, right," I said, recognizing authority and coherence (of which I was incapable, with my mouth full of tongue).

"We have to get to the . . . ah . . . ha-hospital right nooows!" He'd already roared away; we followed in hot pursuit. I'm surprised he didn't give me a Breathalyzer test, but he'd doubtless seen a lot of erratic behavior from nervous fathers. Thanks to him, I got there before my son did, but not by a whole lot. I had an hour or so in the labor room, holding my girl's hand. . . . I hope useful for her, as it surely was for me. Of course, fathers were banned from the actual birth in those days; I was banished to the lobby with the other anxious dads, leaving Lydia and Fray to work it out together. (I remember passing another imminent mother, strapped to a gurney, waving her arms overhead and announcing firmly, "Wait a minute here. I'VE CHANGED MY MIND!!")

I'm afraid I dozed off again in the next hour or so (I'd had a tough day, though obviously not as tough as my girl's). Still, I'll never forget the blooming happiness that spread in me like the sun coming up when Lydia's obstetrician poked me awake: "Congratulations . . . you have a fine son."

I ran back to find Lydia exhausted and sweating but triumphant, our little male bear cub sleeping serene in her arms. Of course I blew my next responsibility, too. Calling the family, I said to my father, "Congratulations! You're the grandfather of a seven-pound, fourteen-and-a-half-boy ounce!"

There was a slight pause, then my dad said, "Gee, I was hoping for a baby."

That was a generation ago. Now, Fray's taller than I am. At birth, his son looked even more like a bear cub than he had, with a thick thatch of bristling black hair and alert black eyes as big as olives (which turned blue in days, an inheritance from my Scots grandfather, as was his ultimately blond hair). We got to the hospital less than an hour after he was born. Still dressed in the surgical greens he'd worn to help his son into the world, Fray brought him from the nursery into Marilyn's room, where she sat, glowing with happiness. We were all glowing . . . and not from the Lanson champagne in which we toasted the new member of the clan.

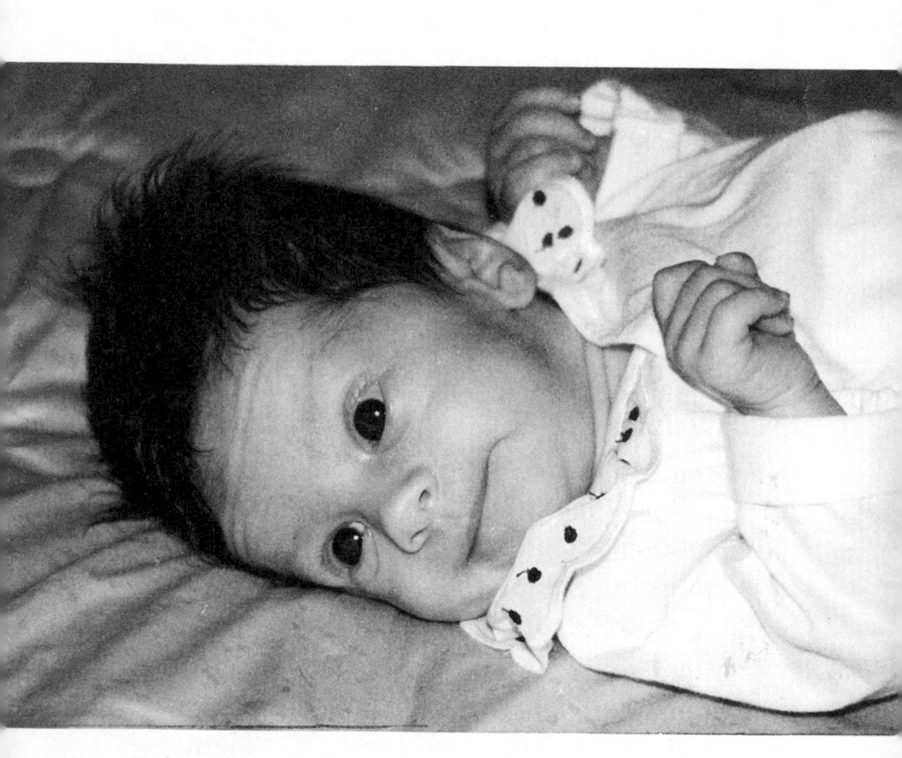

Jack aged 6 months.

Driving back from the hospital on the first morning our grandson would see, I said to Lydia, "You know, this is sort of a chance to go back and live part of our lives over again. Almost a second time around."

She took my hand. "Maybe as good as the first." And so it has been. Sometimes life drops blessings in your lap, without your lifting a finger. Serendipity, they call it. Home again, we sat on the terrace steps to watch the sun come up, as we hadn't done for thirty years, when there was an Oscar in my lap. Believe me, a grandson is better.

Early in the New Year, we gathered our friends at the house for Jack's christening. I put a carved cedar bar stool draped in white linen in the front patio and dug out a sterling-silver punch bowl as a font. God gave us a warm, clear day; a fine Episcopal priest, Peter Kreitler, took over from His hands and named our boy "John Alexander Clarke," honoring godfather and grandmother and no doubt marking the last time in his life he'd be called "John."

Jack's role was passive, but he followed events with interest, smiling angelically at the applause, retiring briefly for a meal and a wardrobe change, then ended the day sleeping happily in the arms of his great-grandmother, Lilla Heston. My mother hadn't been to the Coast for more than a year, though she'd always loved to travel. At 94, it was getting too difficult for her, but she was determined to be there for Jack's christening. It was her last trip. In a little over a year, she was gone . . . but she'd held her great-grandson in her arms, as, half a century earlier she'd held me, then Fray and Holly.

My toast at the end of the day was the same I'd spoken for my firstborn, from Genesis: "The smell of my son is as the smell of a field which the Lord hath blessed." As the seasons turned and Jack grew, I suddenly realized he was free of a danger that had hung over his father, and all of us, almost all of Fray's life: the threat of a Soviet nuclear attack. Their empire had just collapsed, the Berlin Wall was down. Whatever dangers Jack may face, they won't include a mushroom cloud.

There's a silly cliché about grandparentage. "Oh, it must be great," people say. "All the fun, and none of the responsibility!" It's surely great,

Lydia Heston holding newborn Jack.

but I feel as strong a responsibility for Jack when he's with me as ever I did with our children. That's part of what I said to Lydia, the morning Jack was born . . . the chance to do it all again.

Of course, Jack came into the world already equipped with parents, well able and eager to raise him . . . but we were ideally situated to lend a hand. Our two houses are only one canyon apart, along the spine of low mountains above Beverly Hills, six minutes by car. Fray and Marilyn are very generous in lending Jack for a few hours, even a few days. When Jack was born, both Fray and I were preparing films, so the constant availability of the two households worked out very conveniently. It's also important that both households are interlocked and secure against intruders.

For Jack, too: he's perfectly content in either household. (Excuse me, Mrs. Clinton, but you're dead wrong: It doesn't "take a village to raise a child.") It takes a family. That's what Jack has . . . an extended family. Believe me, there are a lot of functioning families like that in South Central Los Angeles, too . . . even some of those with no dad.

I've kept a work journal all my adult life: The last few years are increasingly crowded with the

Jack (age 4) in our pool.

adventures of Jack. That's what this little book is: the chronicle of a baby becoming a toddler, then stretching into boyhood, and *learning* . . . how to do your best and keep your promises, be fair, but never give up. How to dive a brick up from the bottom of the pool and do your numbers. How to hit something like a backhand volley . . . and above all, how to *read,* and some day grow into a good man.

Already, he's a fine little guy. Some three years ago, beating me yet again in a race down the hall and jumping down three steps to the front patio, he looked at me thoughtfully. "Ba," he said, "are you old?"

"Yeah, Jack," I said. "I'm pretty old."

He reached over and patted my arm. "You're strong, doh," he said firmly. True enough. That's why I want to hang around and act some more . . . and write about Jack. He's strong, too.

CHAPTER ONE

When We Were Very Young

Like his father before him, Jack was on his first film location before his first birthday (though it occurs to me Fray's ahead there: He played the infant Moses for Mr. DeMille at only three months). In 1992, we went to Israel to film a four-hour series I'd prepared on the core stories from both the Old and the New Testaments, in the King James translation, each story to be shot on the ground where it's presumed to have happened.

It turned out to be one of the best things I ever did, but it was a very tough shoot. Happily, the

Me with son Fraser (age 3) Rome, 1958, on *Ben-Hur*. Actor on right is Jack Hawkins. *(Studio photograph)*

prep on his own film being ahead of schedule, Fray was able to be with us for the whole time. As I've told Jack more than once, his daddy's a very good man to have around in a crisis.

Jack, on the other hand, was frustrated. To his intense irritation, he couldn't walk yet, though he scrabbled relentlessly across the carpet in the hotel suite. He couldn't really talk, either. When Marilyn brought him out to location for lunch, he'd run through his repertoire of random sounds in the hope he'd stumble over an actual word. One day, he did. As I swept him up from his stroller, he grabbed my ear, looked at me and said, "BA!"

I took his finger, put it on my nose and asked carefully, "Ba?"

"BAAA!" he shouted, triumphant. "Ba-Ba BAAA!" So it must have been when the first Cro-Magnon struck sparks from flint and made fire. I have been "Ba" to Jack from that day . . . a name I'm proud to bear. When I go in to Jack's kindergarten class to read to them, his classmates call me "Ba," too. That suits me fine. Not long afterward, Jack decided that Lydia's name was "Nana" and so she has been, ever since.

Fraser and Jack Heston (age 4). *(Photo courtesy of Marilyn Heston.)*

Jack (age 4) and simian companion.

Fray gave us an even more telling memory on the Bible shoot. We were filming John's Baptism of Jesus in the River Jordan (which is not a huge river; when I played that part for George Stevens, we used the Colorado). Still, this was the real Jordan. I was standing in it hip deep, waiting for the crew, Fray was sitting on the bank playing with Jack when he noticed Lydia with her camera, searching as ever for the perfect shot. Fray leaped to his feet. "Mom . . . here's what you want."

It was, too. He strode to the river's edge, bent over and dipped Jack's naked feet in the Jordan. Of course it was our Christmas card that year, one of the best of the thirty-some she's done over the years. Roll, Jordan, roll.

Dear Jack:

I think this is the first real letter I've ever written to you, not counting postcards when you're on location with your mom and dad. We see each other all the time, of course. Some of the happiest times I know have been with you . . . swimming, or playing tennis, reading stories, or painting . . . or just talking. You ask very good questions. I've

Jack Heston (age 4) graduates from preschool.

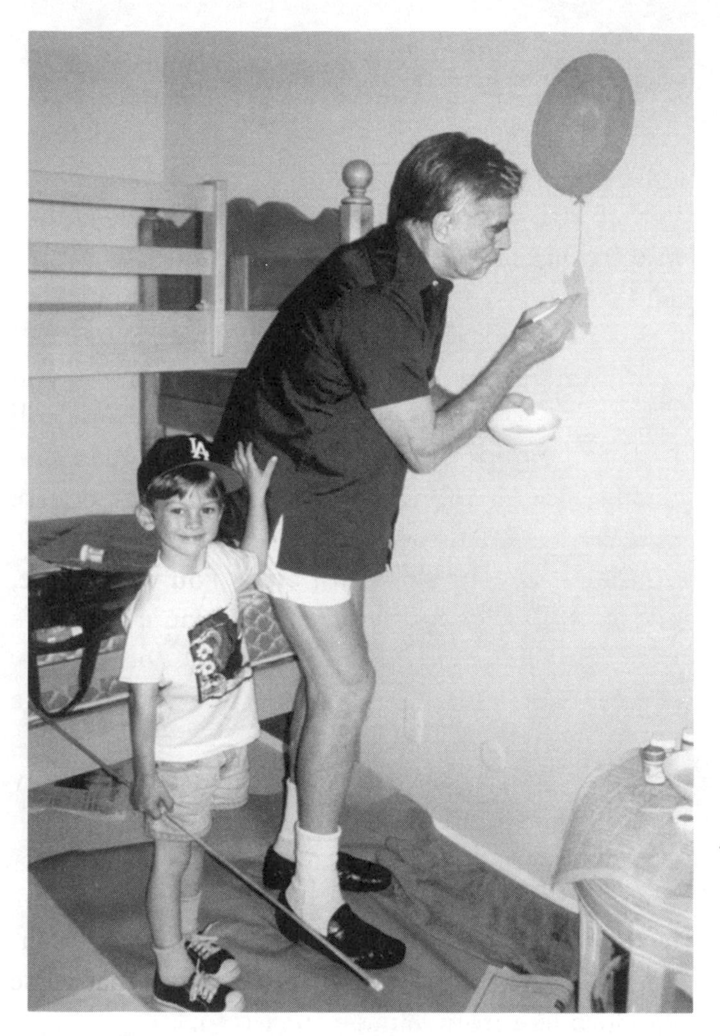

Painting Winnie the Pooh on the walls of Jack's new room.

learned a lot, trying to figure out good answers. ("What are clouds made of, Ba?" "Water; it gets carried up in the sky, where it's cold, and turns into vapor . . . a little like fog. Then it gathers together into clouds." "Yes . . . but what are clouds *for?*") That last one was a toughie, Jack. I think I said something like, "Ohh . . . just for fun, maybe. I think God likes them."

I don't know if you remember that . . . you asked me way last summer, when you were still four. I wrote it down, so I'd remember it. I write down a lot of the things you say, but of course you can't read them, or this letter, yet. I know, you learned your alphabet before you were three, and Nana works on phonics with you every time you come over here to play, but I don't know if you'll be able to read a whole letter for a while yet.

But I thought I'd start writing to you anyway . . . real letters, from me to you, then put them in a book you can read when you're older, with pictures of the things we all saw, so you can remember them. Also the things you and I did together, and talked about. I know you remember that verse we both like from Winnie the Pooh.

"What would I do?" I said to Pooh,
"If it wasn't for you," and Pooh said: "True,
It isn't much fun for One, but Two
Can stick together," says Pooh, says he.
"That's how it is," says Pooh.

That's what we do, Jack. It's a pretty good rule for all your life, really . . . you want to stick with the people you care about.

With Love
Ba!

CHAPTER TWO

I Can Do It Myself!!

The heights by great men reached and kept
Were not attained by sudden flight,
But they, while their companions slept
Were toiling upward, through the night.

— HENRY WADSWORTH LONGFELLOW

There are few tasks undertaken with more tireless ardor than when a two-and-a-half-year-old boy is determined to tie his own shoe. Tugging it onto one foot while hopping around on the other, then endless attacks on the actual double bow knot. "Remember, hold one loop in two fingers, then bring the other over and back up through, and pull them . . ."

"I *had* it then . . . you innarupted me!" The Normandy landings can't have been undertaken with fiercer commitment, nor more relish in the final victory. Learning to put on a pair of tennis shoes and tie a double-bow knot is a major rite of passage for a small boy.

No, I don't think it's the same for little girls. We raised a little girl only five years behind her brother, and I can tell you categorically: They are *not* the same. There was a time in the sixties (not the country's best decade, on several counts) when there was a sturdy band of zealots who insisted boys and girls were in fact identical, though there was no evidence whatever to support this. Certainly not among parents. There may be a few Amazons from N.O.W. who keep that faith still, but they must be lonely.

It's officially known now as "The '94 Quake." It hit at 4:31 A.M., January 17th, shaking us both awake. As transplanted Angelenos, this was our third, and measurably worst, earthquake. I can't say it scared me, though it sure Lord caught my attention. I turned and pulled Lydia into my arms as she awakened, and simply held her, very tightly.

There didn't seem to be much danger, though she was quivering. The room shook, violently but not noisily ("*Very* noisily!" says my girl), for something under thirty seconds (though some later insisted it was at least five minutes, maybe ten). By any measure, the rumbling earth steadied; we got out of bed and found the flashlights . . .

On the downtown skyline you could see huge red flashes blooming in the darkness: I suddenly realised they were generator substations burning out. All power was gone, of course, not just electricity . . . phone lines, gas, radio and TV, the works. We dressed in track suits and running shoes (in case of broken glass) then checked the front room, where there were a couple of hundred books and some fallen sculptures on the floor, but no other damage.

The kitchen was a mess, of course—broken pots and cups crackling under foot—as was the pantry (the bar awash in shattered Lalique glasses). The coffee had made itself minutes before the power went, so we had some, then put the rest in a thermos before it turned cold, then set off for Fray's house, along the route he and I had agreed on long before to minimize the chance of missing each other in dealing with whatever crisis might come up. I put a handgun on the seat beside me, but we didn't see a single car. Mulholland Drive was littered with rocks, water gushing down the canyon the first half mile, but it was passable, though still pitch dark.

We arrived at Fray's just as he'd finished loading his pickup to come to us. "Take Jack a minute, would you?" he said, handing his son to me. "I've been carrying him on one arm and working with the other for nearly an hour." He'd leapt out of bed buck naked, swept son and bedclothes up in one bundle and run downstairs. "Damn fool thing to do," he said. "Suppose there'd been broken glass on the stairs? I'd've had a tough time taking care of Jack with a slashed foot." (Marilyn was away, skiing in Utah.)

Our ridge was clearly our best headquarters, with three of us to watch Jack and stay on alert while we waited for the outside world. So we returned there. As we realized when I dug up a battery-powered radio, we'd been very lucky; many areas and some of our friends had suffered

Jack trying out a bulldozer to repair earthquake damage, 1996.

dreadful damage. There were still occasional aftershocks (the final death toll overall was sixty-two).

Jack seemed perfectly calm, I was pleased to see. I've noticed that children are usually very secure in threatening circumstances, as long as adults they trust are calm. A case in point: It was still dark; I was looking for candles to give us a little illumination when I lost track of Jack somehow. I ran for the front hall, where I found him sitting on a tall Spanish chair with his hands folded in his lap. "What are you doing out here, Jack?" I asked.

"I'n behaving," he explained, looking at me serenely. There was a two-year-old with a sense of when *not* to be a two-year-old.

As the daylight grew, we could measure our losses, which were minimal. I dreaded going down into the library, though. It opens off our bedroom, built down to bedrock, with shelves rising twenty feet around four sides, plus alcoves. I flashed my lantern from the top of the stairs, expecting chaos, but it seemed untouched. I guess it really *was* set in rock. One small section . . .

maybe fifty books, had fallen (I think it was Medieval English History) and one tall sculpture had crashed. Yes. We were very lucky.

I think when you've survived a disaster, you're a little uncertain about what to do next. We'd come through all but intact. Now what? Fray drove over to the studio to check out his offices, finding no damage, though all power was still down, along with the computers. Strangely enough (no, entirely predictably, I guess) I'd done exactly the same thing during the Sylmar quake in 1971. I'd been preparing a film at Warners (*Omega Man,* if you care) and drove in to check the studio . . . just to be doing something remotely useful. My luck was no better than Fray's, twenty years later.

I could've swum with Jack, or hit some tennis balls, but it didn't seem appropriate, with the battery radio producing an endless litany of widening disaster. Our cell phones were working, of course, but we couldn't get any calls through. Later in the afternoon, we became useful as more than lucky survivors. When Simsie and Vance Trussell at last reached us by cell phone, their entire house was an unliveable shambles. With little more than the clothes they wore, Simsie and Vance, their two children, as well as Simsie's mother, our good friend Maggie Field, reached our ridge at about the time Marilyn got back from skiing. She'd had a chill premonition the night before and driven straight through for California, desperately trying in the dawn hours to find a car phone that would answer, but knowing from our firm family plan at least which canyon to come to.

(Oddly, Jack, playing happily in his sandbox by then, refused to talk to her at first, though she soon won him 'round.) Some thirteen hours after the quake, everyone was ravenous, so Fray and Simsie drove down to Mr. Chow's for Chinese take-out (roughing it, Beverly Hills style). We were ten at dinner, which Lydia served on the Minton china, the only service we had left with that many intact plates.

The power and all utilities flicked on as night was falling, just as I was warning our motley crew to light the lanterns. It must've taken a massive effort on the part of just about everyone in the city government to come so nearly back up to normal in half a day. We bedded down four Trussells and Maggie Field among our guest rooms and the sofas in the front room; of course we had bedrooms for Fray's family.

After I'd read Jack the ritual two stories ("Just *one* more, Ba"), I said to him, "You were very brave this morning in the earthquake, Jack. Weren't you scared?"

"Weow . . . maybe a *yiddow* bit." He paused, considering. "But I had my Daddy, of course." At this point Fray came in and picked him up for bed. Of course . . . he had his Daddy.

Dear Jack:

I don't know if you remember the earthquake. Most of us can't remember much that happened when we were two. That quake ruined a lot of houses and even killed some people, but we were lucky. We just had a few things broken and some books bent.

We also planned ahead (you should always try to plan, Jack). Your daddy and I had decided long before which roads we would take between your house and ours if something went wrong, so we couldn't miss each other in the dark. We had extra food and water so we wouldn't be hungry; we also had room for Maggie and Simsie and Vance and their children. When your mommy got back from skiing, she knew to come to our house first. So we were all together.

Even so, you did very well. You didn't cry; you didn't even get upset. Very often, that's what brave is: being calm and figuring out the best thing to do. Your daddy was proud of you; so was I.

Part of being brave is not giving up. You remember what the two kids in your dad's movie *Alaska* said when they were looking for their father? "Never give up, never give up, never give up."

Long before you were born (before your daddy was born), there was a huge and terrible war, started by a very bad man named Hitler. At first he won all the battles, and beat all the countries except England. (Also America, but we couldn't help the English much at first, because some other bad guys in Japan started a war against the United States. That's the war I was in.) You've been to these countries, Jack . . . you can remember a little

Charlton and Jack Heston (age 4) meeting a soldier from the film *Toy Story*, Walt Disney World, Orlando, Florida.

about them. I'll show you on the big globe down in the library.

You can't remember that war, of course, but you should think about it; it was the most important thing that happened in the world in almost a hundred years, since our Civil War (I'll write you about that war later). Hitler was ready to send his armies from France into England, and all there was to stop him were a few hundred young Englishmen (not that much older than you are now, Jack) in fighter planes.

The leader of the English then was a great man named Winston Churchill, who had fought in a war himself, long before. As the English and the Americans waited to see if Hitler could land in England, this is what Mr. Churchill said:

"We shall fight on the beaches, we shall fight on the landing grounds, we shall fight in the fields and in the streets, we shall fight in the hills; we shall never surrender."

They didn't, either. Neither did America . . . and in the end, the good guys won and the bad guys collapsed. (Though that took another forty some years.)

This letter is not about you fighting in the streets, Jack . . . God willing, you'll never have to do that. But you did learn to tie your shoes yourself, and you never gave up. That's a big part of being brave.

Infinite love,
Infinite kisses
Ba.

CHAPTER THREE

Distant Places, Different Faces

The world is so full of a number of things,
I'm sure we should all be as happy as kings.

—ROBERT LOUIS STEVENSON

Actors have always been Gypsies, back several centuries to the time when we wandered around with a wagonload of props and costumes, stopping in a village and doing a play (also the trick with three walnut shells and a pea), then sleeping in a stable and moving on before anyone caught on to the scam with the walnut shells. Personally,

I've never slept in a stable, though I did spend two nights in a sleeping bag on top of Mount Sinai, searching for Moses with Mr. DeMille. (It wasn't that tough . . . DeMille did it and he was forty years older than I was. It's true, making my living, I've moved around an awful lot . . . I've acted on every continent on the globe except Antarctica.

Happily, I've been able to take my family with me to just about all those places. Both Holly and Fray agree it's been a wonderful ride. (Yeah, Jack too, though he's only been along the last three or four years, on both his Daddy's locations and mine.)

Aside from his brief triumph as the infant Moses for Mr. DeMille (of which more later), Fray's first visit to a film location was in Arizona, where I was shooting a western with Anne Baxter called *Three Violent People.* By modern standards, it was not that violent: No brains on the ceiling; everybody who got killed richly deserved it. Unfortunately, it wasn't marvelous, either, though not bad. Certainly Anne was much better as a hoydenish Civil War survivor than she'd been the year before as an Egyptian princess in *Ten Com-*

Teaching Jack to swim, 1992.

Jack (age 2) receives the gold star for swimming lessons, 1993.

mandments. (Never mind . . . nobody can play everything.)

Fray was very happy exploring the pleasures of not-yet-one . . . until I went off on location. There's really no way to explain that kind of separation to a little boy. He still had his mommy and his stuffed animals and lots of smooth carpet to crawl around on . . . but what happened to the big guy with the broken nose, who threw you up in the air and always caught you??

Lydia said he didn't cry, but he spent a lot of time crawling around in my den, looking in the kneehole of my desk and inside my closet. When I phoned at night, he'd listen to my voice, then put his eye to the earpiece, trying to find me.

"Bring him down now, darling!" I said, though we'd planned a later visit. "Maybe he can handle this . . . I don't think I can."

She came the next day. It'd been a long one for me, jumping on and off horses, firing several dozen rounds of blanks at a variety of bad guys. Dirty boots propped on the jump seat in the back of the limo, I'd have slept all the way in to the hotel . . . except that I knew they'd be waiting there.

Unlocking the door, I could hear Lydia giving him his bath. As I stepped in behind them, he was having a raucous-little-boy time splashing in the tub with a rubber duck. "Hey, cowboy," I said.

He looked up at me, his eyes widening, then lowered his head and examined his duck meticulously. I picked him up and held him to me, naked and dripping, but he kept his face buried in my neck. "Hello, boy," I whispered in his ear, my heart swelling as he gripped me tightly with both arms and legs, still not uttering a sound.

Nothing that happened to me all that year meant as much as that passionately needful, speechless welcome from my infant son. It's the most valuable lesson I've ever learned about raising kids. It's very simple: Beyond any other measure, the best thing you can give your child is your time. It's often not easy, sometimes not doable, but it's time you *must* find somehow, and seize, whether you're a senator or a street cleaner. It doesn't matter what you *do* . . . wash the car, hit tennis balls, shop for Mother's Day, as long as you do it together.

Of course the first significant involvement of any of my progeny on a film location had hap-

Marilyn Heston, Jack's mother, in Israel in 1992.

Jack Heston meets his cousin, Ridley Charlton Rochell, with his aunt Holly in California, January, 1997.

pened many months earlier, when Fray played the infant Moses for Mr. DeMille . . . a birth gift, really. When Mr. DeMille learned the expected date of Fray's birth, he realised he would thus be three months old just as we'd be shooting the scenes of the infant Moses. The morning Fray was born, the first message we got in the hospital (at 5 A.M.) was a wire:

CONGRATULATIONS: HE HAS THE PART.
C.B. DEMILLE.

Fray's screen debut seemed to disturb him not at all . . . he viewed the world with serene detachment, confident he'd be fed, dry, and warmly held at appropriate intervals. As a fledgling actor, he also had a distinguished cast of costars in his few scenes: Martha Scott, Nina Foch, and Judith Anderson, plus a bevy of beautiful Egyptian ladies-in-waiting. Who could ask for anything more?

Of course the whole undertaking was under the firm control of the California Department of Labor. Since babies of three months can only work under the lights for one hour total on any given day, with no take longer than forty-five seconds, only six takes permitted in any one hour, and all this to be accomplished in not more than three hours on the lot, the shooting was scheduled with meticulous focus on Fraser's convenience. Lydia had to be there, of course, as a walking dairy (meal breaks were at the option of the actor, who was unpredictable). There were also the usual pit stops for wardrobe change . . . also unpredictable.

We'd done some long shots during the Egyptian location of the closed basket drifting down the real Nile; now they'd built a little estuary on a sound stage at Paramount, complete with genuine papyrus reeds, and the covered basket, which floated very seaworthily. There was also a rather formidable nurse, hired at the behest of the California Department of Labor. When all was ready, she plucked Fray from his mother's arms and strode to the edge of the landing. I was already in the water, hovering in a supervisory sort of way. I waded over and reached up for my son. "I'll take him." The nurse tightened her grip.

"Oh, no, sir," she said. "I have to handle him during all filming." I looked at her with only a little less candlepower than I turned on Yul Brynner in the confrontation scenes with Pharaoh.

"Give . . . me . . . that . . . child," I said softly.

She turned pale and handed him over, stumbling back. I deposited him in the basket, where he seemed quite content, and closed the lid as the cameras turned. Nina, as Pharaoh's daughter, knelt and opened it, projecting wonder. I was wondering, too: Why did the basket seem . . . lower, somehow? As the take ended, I saw Fray was actually floating, while the basket slowly sank under him. I plucked him from the water, still cool and calm, as he remains to this day.

The baby Moses was his last performance, alas. He retired and put his salary into Paramount stock, where it has multiplied, like the Children of Israel. Fray toils now behind the camera as a director, where he often has to make bricks without straw.

Over the next ten or fifteen years, he had an extraordinary exposure to filmmaking before he even knew what it was. At age two, he met Walt Disney, who, on being informed that Fray had seen *Perri* four times, squatted beside him and asked his opinion of the hawk eating the squirrel. "Weow . . . he was jus' gettin' his dinner," said my son, the infant film critic. Disney, no fool, was clearly consulting his core audience; Fray merely confirmed what Disney's genius had already taught him . . . hawks get to have dinner, too.

Not long after, shooting a western (*The Big Country*) for William Wyler, I was working a feisty pinto stud they'd picked for me when Lydia brought Fray out to the location. As soon as he saw the horse, he wanted to get on him, an enthusiasm I didn't share. His name was Domino, and he was just this side of being too much horse for me; I wasn't wild about risking my firstborn on him as well.

Of course Fray won me over (as my children and grandchildren have often done). I swung him up on the pommel in front of me, tucking his heels under the tack, and off we went, just about as fast as I was willing to let that horse run. As I eased Domino down to a light canter, Fray patted my right hand, which was holding him close. "Don't worry, Daddy," he said. "You won't fall off."

An odd thing: I've had to type the above paragraph twice. I kept writing "Jack," instead of "Fray." It's not surprising, I suppose: They're

Jack (age 5) on horseback. *(Photo courtesy of Marilyn Heston.)*

very much alike; just about everything I remember Fray doing, I can imagine, if not recall, Jack doing also, thirty years after.

Our next major location, or dislocation really, was the *United States*, the fastest and one of the very best of the big liners that carried us over the Atlantic on this first of a number of voyages I took to far shores over the next several years in pursuit of my living. Those great ships are long gone now, surrendered to the 747s endlessly circling the globe, and the cruise ships (which are not the same, believe me).

As we very soon came to appreciate, the liners were truly the best way to travel. About the second day out, Fray said to me as we were paddling around the shallow end of the pool, "I *wike* dis ship, Daddy. You don't have any innaviews an' no rehearsals . . . just da captain's cocktail party." My sentiments exactly (though the captain did expect black tie at his party).

Over the next decade, I made several films in Italy, Spain, and England. We traveled to all of them on the big liners, even then in the twilight of their dominance. Our daughter, Holly, had joined us by then and enjoyed several voyages, which she recalls in surprising detail for the toddler she was then. She firmly insists that her happiest memory of her first voyage on the *Queen Mary* was that she had mandarin oranges at every meal. Not the rich, rolling swell of the vast Atlantic in perfect weather, not that great ship, slicing through the dark, foam-crested waves. Just "baby oranges" at every meal.

Our wonderful seaborne isolation on that first voyage to the *Ben-Hur* shoot came to a jarring halt when we docked at Southampton. From the moment we cleared immigration, running a press gauntlet to the limo carrying us north to London, I began an endless series of interviews that continued, when I was not actually on the set filming, until *Ben-Hur* was in the theaters a year and a half later. I know, that's part of what they pay me for and I try to do it well, but out of seventy-several movies, I don't recall anything like the media frenzy that surrounded that shoot. It must've been those white horses.

MGM also needed a day or so of wardrobe tests in London, and I've always been glad to spend time in that greatest and most glorious of cities in the world. Samuel Johnson was right: "The man who is bored with London is bored with life." Lydia and I saw some plays, and I had time to take Fray to the London Zoo, adding to his international collection of great zoos, before we took off for Paris, where we'd entrain for Rome. In the Tuilleries, pursued by *Paris Match,* I tried to take my son on a small merry-go-round, whose owner, spotting the cameras and my public face, insisted we were planning to shoot footage for the chariot race in the film.

Fray just wanted to ride a merry-go-round, the *Paris Match* photogs wanted a few shots of *Ben-Hur*'s son on a wooden horse, and the plump French lady who owned the merry-go-round was greedily dreaming of instant riches. We were all disappointed, though Fray was the only one who wept, and he was barely three years old.

I chased off *Paris Match,* and closed the limo door on the French lady's imprecations, and headed back to the hotel. "Hey, cowboy," I whispered in his ear, tasting his tears, "I promise you . . . and you know I always keep my promises . . . I *promise* you when we get to Rome and I learn how to drive the chariot, I will take you for a ride in it."

I did, too, though it took me more than a month before I could handle that white team alone. Once we started actually filming the race sequence, it became one of the major tourist attractions in Rome, even rivalling St. Peter's, I do believe. A pass to the Cinecittà back lot, where MGM had re-created the Great Circus of Antioch, was a very hot ticket all that summer.

The bolder of our friends visiting the set took a lap around the track with me, as did many of the frequent VIPs, and of course Lydia, but Fray was a dauntless and tireless passenger. The charioteer needs both hands free for the reins, but he fitted neatly between my knees, gripping the front rail manfully, just able to see over it, yelling encouragement to the horses over the overwhelming thunder of the arena.

When I told this story to Fray's son a while ago, Jack said wistfully, "Dey don't have dose horses anymore, do dey, Ba?" I realized that he was trying to deal, perhaps for the first time, with the sense of loss . . . of something wonderful that once was, and now is not. Gone forever. Besides, the thrilling reality we'd made was only for a movie; that chariot race's permanent claim to being the best action sequence ever filmed, not least because Wyler managed to personalize its desperate havoc, has no place in the real world.

"No, Jack," I said, "that was long ago, when your Daddy was younger than you are. They don't have those horses now and it would cost too much money to make that movie again. I don't want you to see it yet, anyway, certainly not on video. But when you're a year or so older, we'll get a print of the real movie and run it out in our screening room, for you and your friends." I do think he understood what I was trying to say. He's a bright little boy.

When I finished the *Ben-Hur* shoot, a stone rolled off my chest. It was, and remains, one of the most difficult films I've ever made, partly because it was so long, with me in almost every scene, partly because of William Wyler's rock-solid determination to get it absolutely right . . . particularly me. We did pretty well, winning a plethora of prizes (only some of them meaningful), culminating in eleven Academy Awards, more than any film has ever won, or is likely to again.

We sailed for the U.S. out of Naples on an

American liner, the *Independence.* As we boarded on A Deck, we passed a wonderful carved bust of the Indian Chief Seneca. I felt instantly at home.

A cold is the actor's prime nemesis. I never catch one during a shoot, but, as I expected, the monster cold that had been lying in wait for ten months struck me the first day out of Naples. I didn't really care; the work was finished; I wasn't using the equipment that week anyway. Fray and I had a marvelous time exploring the ship (thanks to the captain's courtesy) from engine room to bridge.

The memory of that homeward journey I treasure most, though, is when we reached equatorial waters off Brazil. Fray and I were lying on towels at the base of one of the main stacks. I was making up stories to entertain him, but waiting for noon, when I knew the ship would turn sharply ninety degrees north, setting a course for New York. At sea, it looks as though the sun, not the ship, has moved. As the noon bell struck and the ship turned, I said, pointing to the sun, "Watch this, Fray."

He was enchanted to see the sun suddenly swing overhead, across the arc of the sky. With touching confidence that this was my personal miracle, he said, "Do it again, Daddy!"

Fray is of course long past surrendering to the sweet deceptions we use to entertain and enlighten our children. I was pleased, though, to see I could make the sun move one more time with Jack. A couple of years ago, we all went down to San Diego, where one of the last of the full-rigged ships, *The Star of India*, is moored, still seaworthy and flawlessly maintained by a dedicated crew of volunteers. She puts to sea a few times every year. We had the privilege of joining her on a daylong off-shore cruise.

Fray, an ardent sailor, spent most of his time high in the rigging, willing himself back into Nelson's navy, while Lydia and Marilyn ran their cameras. That left me with the Jack-watch, a role with which I was very happy. The two of us explored several imaginary archipelagos in a dugout canoe on display in a modest and quite deserted maritime museum they had below decks. ("Cast off, mate, for the love o' God! If those scoundrels see we have their longboat, they'll fire on us from the fort! That twelve-pounder could blow us to splinters! Pull, man, PULL!!")

Jack and I on board the ship *Star of India* San Diego, California, 1993. *(Photo courtesy of Marilyn Heston)*

I'd checked with the skipper; when it came close to noon, I took Jack topside, and we sat on some coiled lines on the quarter deck. It wasn't déjà vu: I was actually repeating that earlier time I'd had with Fray, decades before. "Watch the sun, Jack," I said, pointing up through the rigging, as the tall ship came about and headed back to port. And of course for Jack, as it had been for his father years earlier, it was the sun that moved. Yes, like his Dad, he crowed, "Again, Ba!!" This is a small story, really, but it's the stuff from which families build their memories.

The crosshatched counterpane of memory over which I've been leading you back and forth, tracing my footsteps and my family's over a couple of generations should give you a clue: I'm having a wonderful time, still trying to get it absolutely right, which is impossible in my trade, but still, every so often, coming pretty close, doing some really good work. At the same time, we've all grown, and learned. Lydia and I know more or less where we're going, working on opposite ends of the camera (she's a still photographer, which means she's her own boss). Fray is vigorously pursuing his muse as a director, which means he has the best job in films.

Holly is happily married and (not many days from when I began this paragraph) about to produce her own child. No, we don't know which kind yet. I'm hoping for a baby. Our family seems to follow certain patterns, like the seasons turning. Holly's baby will be five years younger than Jack, as Holly was five years younger than her brother.

Jack's not a baby anymore . . . barely still a little boy. But to see him growing, learning; to spend some time walking beside him down the same paths his father walked, moving towards manhood, is a very rich experience for me. How rich? Like dancing with Mr. Shakespeare; it doesn't get any better than that.

Resonating through it all, of course, is the sense that things have happened before. Several weeks into the *Ben-Hur* shoot, I got back to the villa we were living in to find the household in an uproar. Fray had somehow locked himself into one of the bathrooms and was beginning to sound a little panicky. The local fire brigade was on the point

Riding the elephant at Ringling Bros. and Barnum & Bailey circus: Jack with his grandfather.

of axing the elaborately carved door down, which seemed to me to present numerous negative possibilities, not least for Fray. When he heard my voice through the door, he settled down enough for me to tell him just the way to turn the very large key in the very large lock. When the door swung open, his lips were quivering. "Boy," he said, "I thought I'd never see America again."

Thirty-odd years later, Jack was also stranded, though not quite as desperately. I was to pick him up from his karate lesson and bring him to our ridge, where his father would collect him in due course. I had a meeting on some project which ran over enough to make me nearly half an hour late at the karate studio, the boys gone home, the karate master at his desk doing paperwork. Jack was sitting alone on a bench in the corner, looking more than a little forlorn. When he saw me, he leaped to his feet. "I knew you'd come, Ba. I said that to myself. You always come." Lord, how they can touch your heart.

Our family has seen a lot of the world together, knocking around several dozen locations over many dozen years, via camels and canoes, helicopters and houseboats, old biplanes and balloons.

Filming can be interesting to watch, but we also got to climb the Great Pyramid at dawn and go into the Roman Coliseum by moonlight (both adventures now forbidden to visitors).

Throughout all this, Lydia's been a one-woman Ministry of Tourism, scheduling Fray and Holly, now Jack as well, on a variety of excursions, museums and great collections of wonderful things, exploring it all. Fray coined the phrase for it when he was about ten: "Are we going ruin-running today, Mom?" Most days, they were.

A few years ago, there was a good TV series, *Young Indiana Jones,* exploring the adventures of that remarkable character at the age of fourteen. Fray, discussing the show with some other filmmakers of his generation, commented, "You know, that was my life when I was a kid . . . doing my school work in hotel suites, exploring scientific digs, the Great Barrier Reef, Hadrian's Wall."

"You mean you're Indiana Jones?" one of his friends asked. Fray grinned. "Nope . . . my Mom is."

"Distant Places, Different Faces," I called this chapter (more or less at random). I didn't realize, perhaps because I'd never thought much about it, how accurately that defined my life and my work . . . and, so, to a large degree, my family as well.

I think what interests me more than anything else—as I rummage through my memories of my children, and now with Jack, exploring the strange world in which I live and do the work that bought all their shoes—is how often their own experiences seem to overlap . . . thirty-odd years apart.

As I was working on this chapter, we got the happy news that we are grandparents again. Our daughter, Holly, has produced a lovely baby girl (as I'd been sure she would from the beginning). It just seemed to fit the pattern of our family. Fraser and Marilyn had a boy; Holly and Carlton would have a girl.

Even the naming of both children followed the family example: Jack Alexander Clarke Heston was balanced neatly by Ridley Charlton Rochell. My mother would've surely been pleased to have another Charlton in the family. James Charlton was my great-grandfather, a lone English boy who came to America and thrived, as so many somehow managed to do then, with no help from anyone. I'm proud my new granddaughter bears his name, even if it is hard to spell. (Over the last few years, I've gotten a surprising number of birth announcements from people who've christened their sons Charlton. I find that touching.)

The other side of my family were Scots ... Clan Fraser. You have to understand that the Scots have been for centuries an angry and difficult people. When the Romans conquered Britain, we were still painting ourselves blue and fighting naked. Finally, the Emperor Hadrian built a wall across all of northern Britain and manned it with two full Roman legions, solely to keep my ancestors on the other side. It didn't work. When the Romans left, the Scots were still there (though we *had* stopped painting ourselves blue).

The most famous and probably the best Fraser of this century is Simon, Lord Lovat, the Macshimi (head) of the clan, who led the British Commandos ashore on Sword Beach in the Normandy landings in World War II, carrying only a swagger stick, with his piper beside him. I knew him only slightly, but he seems to me the kind of man anyone would choose for a father, a grandfather, a son ... or a friend (or a man to follow into battle, surely).

I'm afraid the best known of all the Frasers is

Simon the Fox, the Macshimi who led the Brits a merry chase after the Scots lost the Battle of Culloden in the mid-eighteenth century. Snared at last, he was thrown in the Tower of London and condemned to death as a traitor. On his way to the block, he was taunted by a woman in the jeering crowd, "They'll cut yer ugly head off now, ye filthy Scots dog!"

"Aye, so they wull, ye bluddy English bitch," he retorted equably. And so they did. He was the last nobleman executed in Britain, and the last man beheaded in that country. Dubious distinctions, but there they are. We take our family memories where we find them.

In the Highlands, where all Scots are still tied by their heartstrings, survival once meant mainly keeping the horses fed and the swords sharp. I doubt my Scots forebears brought either horse or blade to America, but they did bring the Fraser genes, a very useful asset. They've served the men in our family well . . . the women, too, come to think of it. We've all learned a great deal from the odd corners of the world we've explored. In a few years, I'll have to find out if the newest member of the clan, Miss Ridley Charlton Rochell, agrees.

Dear Jack:

It's sort of funny to be writing you another letter you can't quite yet read, though I know you're reading better and better every day. Every time I hear you going through your phonics work with Nana, I can see how much further you've come. I think you know already how important this is, Jack . . . I've heard your dad talk to you about it. In the world where you're growing up, the most valuable skill you can have is to know how to read and speak and write the English language . . . *well. Very* well.

The language you were born to is a tool that can truly take you to the stars, Jack. All the airplanes and space craft that fly are controlled in English. More and more of the world's work is done in the English language; science, diplomacy, government, business, the military, the arts, too. All this will be more and more true as you grow up. The better your mastery of English, the more you can choose your life . . . and mold it.

Just a couple of weeks ago, I was driving you up here from school and we were playing that word game we like: "I spy with my little eye, something that begins with . . ." and you stopped and said, "Ba . . . who made up talking in the first place?" I didn't answer, because I couldn't think of how to explain it, and, besides, we were at the house by then and went swimming instead.

Now I've thought about it, I guess God must've made up talking, though it doesn't say that in any of those stories I've told you about how he made the heavens and the earth and the sun and the moon and the oceans and all the animals and fishes. He also made a man and called him "Adam." He put him in charge of things, and he decided to let Adam name all the creatures. They couldn't talk, of course, but Adam could, because God wanted him to, I suppose. So Adam named them all, from the elephant down to the ant. Then God made a woman to be with the man, and she could talk, too. Her name was Eve.

People have been talking ever since. In different languages, as it worked out. English is based a lot on Latin, the language of the Romans, who were one of the great peoples of the world. A lot of our words about ships came from the Vikings, who used to raid along the Scottish coasts, just as many of our words about medicine came from the

Arabs, who were the great scientists and doctors of the Middle Ages.

That's one of the great strengths of English; it absorbs words from other tongues in a way that other languages don't seem able to do, which is why English has more words, of course. There are two more reasons for the growth of English: William Shakespeare and the King James Bible. More and more over the last four centuries, both those works have influenced the spread of English around the world. There is no better writing in the world in *any* language, than in these books.

Only last year, when you'd just turned five, I told you the story of Moses' farewell from the King James. You didn't find it hard to understand, except for the end, where Moses has to stay behind when the people he led so long go over the river to the promised land.

"But why did Moses have to die?" you asked.

"I think maybe God decided Moses had done his work," I said.

"Weow, maybe," you said. "But it's still pretty sad. It's a good story, doh." You're right, Jack. It's a wonderful story. And it's part of your birthright.

In ten or twelve years, you'll be deciding what you want to do with your life when you're a man . . . in science, or the arts (maybe they'll be making movies on the moon when you're twenty). None of us can tell now, but you'll be there to find out. Pretty cool, huh?

Your mom and dad . . . Nana and I, too, will point you as well as we can toward the next century. Wherever it is you decide to go, whatever you decide to do, your language and how you use it will help you get there. Don't forget that, Jack.

"I spy, with my little eye, something that begins with 'L' . . . you got it! *'Love'* I love you, JACK."

All my Love
Ba!

CHAPTER FOUR

America, America

Land where my fathers died
Land of the pilgrims' pride
From every mountain side
Let freedom ring.

—SAMUEL FRANCIS SMITH

America! America!
God shed his grace on thee
And crown thy good with brotherhood
From sea to shining sea.

—KATHERINE LEE BATES

It has been said that the invention of the United States of America is the greatest single political act in the history of mankind. I'll sign that, surely. Democracy is a very tricky system of government, full of potholes and land mines for all concerned.

Winston Churchill once said that it was "the worst system of government in the world . . . except for all the others."

"All the others," of course, includes a sorry list of failed political experiments over several centuries, ranging from the bloody Terror of the French Revolution to the slaughters of Hitler, Stalin, and Mao, in ascending order of horror.

I'd rather not dwell on this, OK? I hope some young people will read this book. If we get into Pol Pot and the Tutsi-Hutu conflict (the Rwandan *government,* for that matter), we'll be up to our ankles in blood. Let's look instead at the first roots of democracy. The Greeks took a good shot at it (the first to try, really). The Romans did it better, and longer. The Roman Empire at its height extended from Palestine to Portugal and from Scotland almost to the Sudan . . . and the Roman peace prevailed there (in an area roughly half the size of the United States) for four hundred years, a longer peace than the world has enjoyed since then.

In the turmoil of the eighteenth century, while the Portuguese and the French and the Spanish and the British were struggling to sort out who

Jack (age 5) in the playground of his school.

would be big dog in the New World, the Brits gradually achieved a supremacy on the east coast of North America that would, over the next century, extend around the world.

Then there was suddenly, in the face of what surely must've seemed like manifest British destiny, something like a miracle: the American Revolution.

How could that have happened? What made it possible? An aroused people in arms . . . and a few great men. The combination of those ingredients is what created this country. A bunch of country boys who were willing to hold a rifle and shiver through the bitter winter at Valley Forge because George Washington was there to stand and shiver with them . . . and they trusted him to get them through it. How many leaders would you trust to do that for us today?

We've been blessed since with great commanders who could turn the tide of circumstance and battle: Andy Jackson at New Orleans, throwing back the British one last time; Winfield Scott at Veracruz; Grant and Lee in the Civil War . . . towering figures both, though on opposite sides.

In this century, we've had men like Pershing

and Patton and Nimitz and MacArthur, in wars we came finally to feel we had to go to and had to win. That made two wars on foreign soil in this century that seemed at first not ours to fight, let alone win. As it happened, we did both, both times. Even counting the fearful cost in American blood and national energy, it left us a better world.

The only examples I can think of that showed the same stubborn, never-give-up indomitability are Mao Tse-tung and Chou En-lai, dragging their ragged band of guerillas through the Long March across China to victory. Yet, having won, and overthrown Chiang Kai-shek, their regime deteriorated into a brutal tyranny far exceeding the savage excesses of Hitler and Stalin.

With Nazism destroyed, Soviet Communism emerged as the next threat to peace on the planet, growing over the next forty years as its goals became clearer. There was a great deal of liberal angst spent defending that Socialist paradise, but in the end, with the firm help of the Brits, we prevailed, both ideologically and in the iron logic of military confrontation. It may be, in the end, the only war ever won without a shot being fired.

The revisionist historians would have it otherwise, but it's now generally agreed: It *was* an Evil Empire, there *was* a Cold War . . . and we won. May God grant peace to all of us.

This book is essentially a long letter to Jack, passing on to him what I hope is useful advice. Of course he was a generation away from being born when Fidel Castro asked for and Khrushchev gave to Cuba ballistic missiles aimed at the United States.

Cuba and the Soviets backed down when Jack Kennedy deployed United States naval units in the path of the Soviet ships carrying missiles and Soviet crews to Cuba. Having faltered in the Bay of Pigs, Kennedy redeemed himself and achieved perhaps the finest hour of his shortened presidency (perhaps prodded by his street-tough brother, Robert). The Cuban missile crisis was surely one of the major confrontations of the Cold War.

I well remember coming home early from whatever meeting on whatever film I was preparing, so I could sit my seven-year-old son down on the couch and explain that we might be at war with the Russians within hours and what that would mean to him and to our family. We were, in the classic phrase, eyeball to eyeball with the bad guys. And they blinked.

I've written before in this little memoir about how often events replicate themselves . . . in our family, quite often. The Cuban missile crisis was a generation behind us when Fray called me, only a few weeks ago, up to his hips in prep on his next film. "Can you pick up Jack early from school . . . right now? There are a couple of guys with AK-47s robbing a bank about a mile from his school."

Of course I could, and did, talking my way through several LAPD barricades to get there. (I have an honest face, and a lot of those guys know me.) I had to explain to Jack, as simply as possible, what had happened to put police cars at every intersection: "A couple of bad men tried to rob a bank near your school, but the police came and killed them."

"Good!" said Jack. Now there's Mosaic justice for you.

We seem to have arrived at a crucial point in the

Jack's first trout, caught by him, April 1994.

Fraser and Jack Heston (age 5) in Yellowstone National Park.

Fraser and Jack (age 5) in Yellowstone National Park beside Old Faithful.

Jack (age 5) taking a lesson in fly-fishing from his father.

history of what I do believe is the most successful democracy in the history of mankind's painful progress towards a just and equitable society. That's equity of opportunity, remember, not results. The Founding Fathers, in their prescient wisdom, promised us life and liberty, but not happiness . . . only the chance to pursue it. If even an omnipotent God will not guarantee us happiness, surely we're foolish to count on government to do it.

Still, the American experience, so far, seems the most successful. To the goddess of history, of course, the two centuries of our little experiment in freedom are only an eye-blink . . . but we are still here. We may not always have been able to make democracy spread, but we have made it prosper. This country is still what it has been from the beginning . . . an example to the world: *Men can live free.* In America, democracy works. Not as well as we need it to work, in these angry, contentious times, but we are still, to the rest of the world, the shining door to freedom.

Why? Why is this? Our system? That's part of it, of course, but it's not that alone. Other countries have cherished that dream and seen it crash in flames and tyranny. What then? Are we smarter, more determined? Is it luck, or the grace of God? I think it's in part the land itself . . . that broad swell of continent between those shining seas.

"The land was ours before we were the land's," Robert Frost wrote. Our great writers have chewed on this from our beginnings. Here's F. Scott Fitzgerald: "We have, perhaps uniquely, a special willingness of the heart, a blithe fearlessness . . . a simple yearning for righteousness and justice that ignited in our revolution a flame of freedom that cannot be stamped out. *That* is the living, fruitful spirit of this country."

And Thomas Wolfe: "It is a fabulous country . . . the only fabulous country, where miracles not only happen, they happen all the time."

And, with towering eloquence, Thomas Paine: "These are the times that try men's souls. The summer soldier and the sunshine patriot will, in this crisis, shrink from the service of their country; but he that stands it *now,* deserves the love and thanks of man and woman."

And finally, Mr. Lincoln, defining America as he so often did: "The last, best hope of earth."

And ". . . with firmness in the right, as God gives us to see the right, let us . . . finish the work we are in, to bind up the nation's wounds."

Lincoln spoke from the cauldron of conflict that was the greatest test to our unity the nation has ever faced . . . the Civil War. There were dreadful losses on both sides . . . and all of them were Americans . . . killing each other.

"We . . . cannot escape history," Lincoln said. "[We] will be remembered in spite of ourselves. . . . The fiery trial through which we pass will light us down in honor or dishonor to the last generation." And, "The dogmas of the quiet past are inadequate to the stormy present. We must think anew and act anew. We must *disenthrall* ourselves . . . and then we shall save our country."

And we did, thanks to Mr. Lincoln. He freed the slaves, found ways and men to win the war, and was shot in the head for his efforts. There've been tens of thousands of men who died for this country; Lincoln is the only president who gave his life "that this nation might live." I'm sure he'd have accepted that bargain gladly.

"With malice toward none, with charity for all," he'd said a few months before he was killed.

"We are not enemies, but friends. We must not be enemies." Somehow, after his death, perhaps to some extent because of his death, the country began to come together again. Not overnight, but over time, the warring entities, Union and Confederate, blended again into the nation, America. Surely, Abraham Lincoln, sixteenth president of the United States, is everlasting in the memory of his countrymen.

Now, nearly a century and a half later, we've been through two world wars we really had to win and six or seven smaller conflicts, some of which we'd have been wise to avoid. That's what Fitzgerald was talking about: this country's "special willingness of the heart." Since the Civil War, almost all our troops were committed to foreign soil, not at home.

I suddenly remember Teddy Roosevelt's maxim: "Speak softly and carry a big stick." Through the eighties, we carved out the bigger stick, the Soviets dropped theirs, and the world was spared a nuclear conflagration that could have sent us all back to the Dark Ages. Now my grandchildren, and yours, can grow up without a mushroom cloud in their future.

So here we are, the sole superpower on the planet, with less inflation and unemployment than any of the developed nations. (Yeah, I know, you're not supposed to use phrases like that, lest the undeveloped nations feel bad.) But we, as Americans, are the ones who should feel bad. Given all the rich bounties of our vast and blessed land and the example of the generations that founded our country and made it the envy of the world, we find ourselves sinking into a rogue culture that's shredding the fabric of the nation that Lincoln described as "man's last, best hope on earth."

I was a little kid in the Depression, the most severe in anyone's living memory. There was relief food available from the Feds, but many families, like ours, "wouldn't take handouts." When the Japanese attacked us and a two-hemisphere war sent thirteen million American men to fight around the world, the people we left at home, building the planes and ships and tanks and growing the crops, just tightened their belts another notch. There was no welfare program on the home front in World War II. Where did that ethic go?

Where, for that matter, did our public schools go? I had the good luck to attend what was rated the finest public high school in the country, but the American public school system overall was then considered the finest *in the world.* That system is now a shambles, often with more bureaucrats than teachers, designed to drag a kid through with a dumbed-down program he cannot fail (lest his self-esteem be damaged).

Where on earth did we get this debate on "instilling self-esteem?" You can't *make* someone feel better about himself. You give him the opportunity and circumstance, and let him seize the day. "Carpe diem."

This is true even more in the colleges and universities, now committed to "diversity" above all, coupled with fail-safe curriculae. They're focussed now on Orwellian social conditioning. I read that Williams College, once highly rated among Ivy League schools, now requires female students to shower in unisex bathrooms, to "make them more comfortable with their bodies." And that male heterosexual students are required to stand on street corners and proclaim themselves homosexuals "so they'll know what it feels like."

These random samples of the state to which education at every age level has fallen in this country are so extreme as to suggest a conscious plan to dismantle the cultural fabric of the country. I cannot believe that, but I do believe teachers' unions are more concerned with tenure, and protecting jobs in the face of appalling incapacity, than they are in teaching students desperately in need of, at the very least, literacy in English.

Though the collapse of the schools is the most important failure in our culture, disabling the next generation, we also see widening fissures everywhere in our society. George Orwell's *1984* was written in 1948, shortly after he'd abandoned his early Marxist enthusiasms. It's intended as black comedy, but Orwell could not have imagined how his dark joke has materialized into reality. Orwell's "Ministry of Truth," dealing only in lies, is reflected today at every level of government and academia with a multitude of "affirmative action" programs that in fact are grossly discriminatory and an array of "diversity requirements" granting privilege to a whole spectrum of groups clamoring for special treatment, based on their ethnicity, their gender (variously defined), their age, and whatever circumstance they feel may qualify them for taxpayers' money. Their agenda is not recognition, nor tolerance, but special status and power.

Each of these contending groups is wrestling for tax dollars, of course, but for status even more. Somewhere in the busy pipeline of public funding is sure to be a demand from a disabled lesbian on welfare that the Metropolitan Opera stage her rap version of *Carmen* as translated into Ebonics.

Another plague upon the land, as devastating as the locusts God loosed on the Egyptians, is "Political Correctness." It colors almost every conversation, certainly every public statement; you cannot now say "him" without adding the anxious "or her." I have no clue what purpose these endless circumlocutions of the language serve, save to confuse. One last example: an early usage, soon laughed off the screen, was "personhole" for "manhole." Can't we just throw away all this nonsense? "Person" is a gray and ugly word anyway. I'm a man, my grandson's a boy, half of you reading this are women and girls. Please, can't we be content with that?

Far more important than any of these rips in

the fabric of American life is the steady erosion of the body politic . . . the way we treat each other. Of course, as always, it begins with the children. We must bring them back to the time we remember; not only your parents, your teachers, but all authority figures, police, clergy, and all those who shape our lives were regarded as compasses to guide us through the morass of adolescence.

Jack takes a karate class three days a week. Aside from the stern physical workout he gets, I'm impressed by the social discipline the karate master imposes. Every one of the dozen or so boys in the class must obey the rules. You cannot speak without raising your hand, you must always address the karate master as "Sir," and you must always obey his orders. *"Thank you, Sir!"* When I was a kid in school, that was a given; there was no question who was in charge. If we can't get back to that, we lose that generation forever. One small karate class, however fiercely disciplined, will only reach a dozen kids. We must somehow instill these values in every school, every class. Then (Mr. Lincoln again): We must *disenthrall* ourselves . . . and then we shall save our country.

My birthday gift, 5-pound weights.

Only a few months ago, a recent heavyweight boxing champion decided to join the Marines . . . and quit after three days, finding the training too tough. *QUIT!!?* That would've been inconceivable for Joe Louis or Jack Dempsey. It would've been impossible in World War II or the Depression. So what has changed?

The idea of America, for one. For more than two hundred years, we've been accepting a constant flood of immigrants (including my ancestors on both sides) who wanted to be part of the freest nation on earth. Now, oddly, we find immigrants eager to accept our largess (welfare, etc.) without quite embracing the country. A century ago, thousands of Italians, Jews, and Germans landed on our shores, a decade or so after my Scots/English ancestors. These latecomers had the added burden of learning the language, which they did with the fierce concentration necessity imposes. (Thank God there was no bilingual program available.) The mantra in all those struggling households was "Speak English! We're in America now!"

Today, most of a century later, new immigrants (many illegal) stumble with English, because *they don't have to learn it;* hundreds of teachers are paid with American tax money to try to educate them in the language of their parents . . . Spanish, Vietnamese . . . Inupiat, too, I don't doubt.

But the saddest plight of all is that of our black children. Blacks make up ten percent of our population, almost all of them from families that have been in America for five or more generations and subject to decades of discrimination at every level. Then, starting in 1961, the Civil Rights movement enfranchised our black citizens . . . I was proud to be part of that noble undertaking long before it became popular in Hollywood. In 1964, I was in the Senate gallery when Hubert Humphrey, the sponsor of the Civil Rights act, assured the Senate that it included no quotas, preferential treatment, nor set-asides for blacks. Of course the next thirty years produced thousands of pages of legislation mandating precisely all of those things.

Never mind! The country and the Congress have drawn back from the excesses of that time, but black Americans have still properly achieved success in every aspect of American life. In sports, business, politics, entertainment, the military, academia, we see gifted and able black men and women assuming significant roles in our society. So it should be.

Still . . . what about the children? Various school districts have tried every conceivable solution . . . integrated schools, all-black schools, all-girl schools, all-boy schools, with and without uniform dress codes. The harsh fact remains: Black children are not doing as well as they should in *any* school, not coming near what their parents did. Why is this? I have absolutely no idea . . . but someone had better figure it out *soon.* What we're struggling with now is a sorry, appalling mess.

There's another factor that figures large in this equation. I suggest that we ignore it at our peril. There are some groups, each with a strong agenda, that are challenging the basic idea of this country . . . One nation.

There's a resourceful public relations guy who, thirty years ago, invented a black African Christmas-time festival, "Kwanzaa." At least in Los Angeles, it's recognized every year, though of course black churches are among the most fervent celebrants of Christmas as the birth of Jesus. There are also a good many Black Muslims, most of whom live in harmony with their Christian neighbors. We also have Louis Farrakhan, whose harsh, anti-Semitic beliefs need no repeating here. There is indeed something to be said for "connecting with others." That connection, though useful, is tough for Christians, or Jews, reaching to the Rev. Farrakhan. May the effort prosper still, though his divisive and blatantly racist comments don't help much.

There is also the curious addiction among many Americans to identify themselves with their roots in another country, another century. Europeans don't do this; when they've joined us, they've joined us. When I began picketing for civil rights in the early sixties, "blacks" was the proper noun. Sorry . . . I can't accept "African-American." I don't think Dr. King would've done so either. (And I was there.)

A far more offensive locution is that chosen by the more aggressive American Indian activists: "Native American." *I'm* a Native American. I'm also, as it happens, a blood brother of the Miniconjou Sioux, memorialized in a blood ritual on Sioux land in South Dakota in 1951. I'm very proud of that but even prouder of the fact that my grandson, Jack, is a thirteenth-generation

Another gift from "Ba," a real wristwatch.

American. His eleven greats grandmother landed in Boston in 1633, her husband having died at sea, with four children and no friends in the New World. They survived and thrived. I doubt that any tribal American Indian has a recorded genealogy in this country approaching Jack's.

They are far too many groups in America as it is, each shouldering the others aside, screaming for special attention, separate identity, to have their disparate diseases moved up in the chain for special funding, possibly even cabinet status, or at least a monument on the Mall, even further obscuring Mr. Lincoln's view from his quiet memorial to George Washington's perfect and simple obelisk.

I say, no more statues, no more memorials. Move them out to Virginia, yes, including the World War II Memorial. That was my war. I know who was in it, so does my family, so do the families of the tens of thousands of good men who died winning it.

Still, as Mr. Lincoln said at Gettysburg: "We cannot dedicate—we cannot consecrate—we cannot hallow—this ground. The brave men, living and dead, who struggled here, have consecrated it far above our poor power to add or detract." I don't think the World War II vets want a damn memorial on the Mall. We did what they asked us to do, we won, and the lucky ones came home. We don't need a memorial to us there, or to the first woman elected to the Congress, or the first man to die of AIDS.

Please, let us leave the Mall, the last free stretch of greensward in our capital, to Mr. Lincoln and Mr. Washington and the American kids who want to kick a football there. That's what it was all about in the first place, making a free country.

We seem to have slid a long way from what the Founders had in mind. "One nation, under God, indivisible, with liberty and justice for all." If we retreat from that, if we fall back into little enclaves of this religion, that language or race, the other set of beliefs, then we're nothing, we're Albania, Bosnia, Zaire!

Not long ago I went to one of those A-list parties I mostly try to avoid, because there were a couple of people there I wanted to talk to. I found myself in a discussion with a beautiful and famous actress I will not embarrass by identifying, about the invention of America and the crucial significance of a single, unified nation. "Well," she said. "Look at the money . . . what it says on the dollar bill. 'E pluribus unum'; from one, many. Right?"

"Actually," I said, as gently as I could, "you've got it backwards. That translates from the Latin as 'From many, one . . . as in one nation."

"No kidding?" she replied, seeming to spend an actual moment exploring the point. "Well . . . whatever," showing her enchanting smile. I didn't argue, reluctant to shoot fish in a barrel, but I remain stunned that an articulate, at least modestly educated woman should be totally ignorant of the principles we've spent more than two centuries defending, at the cost of so much sweat and blood. God help us. (With luck, He might.)

Dear Jack:

I think you're learning to read faster than I'm learning to write. Here I am, plugging along trying to tell you and the people who're printing this book (also the people I hope will read it) how exciting it is to watch you grow up . . . and all the time, you're growing up faster than I can keep track.

Rehearsal night for the school show: Jack takes a bow.

(Photos courtesy of Marilyn Heston)

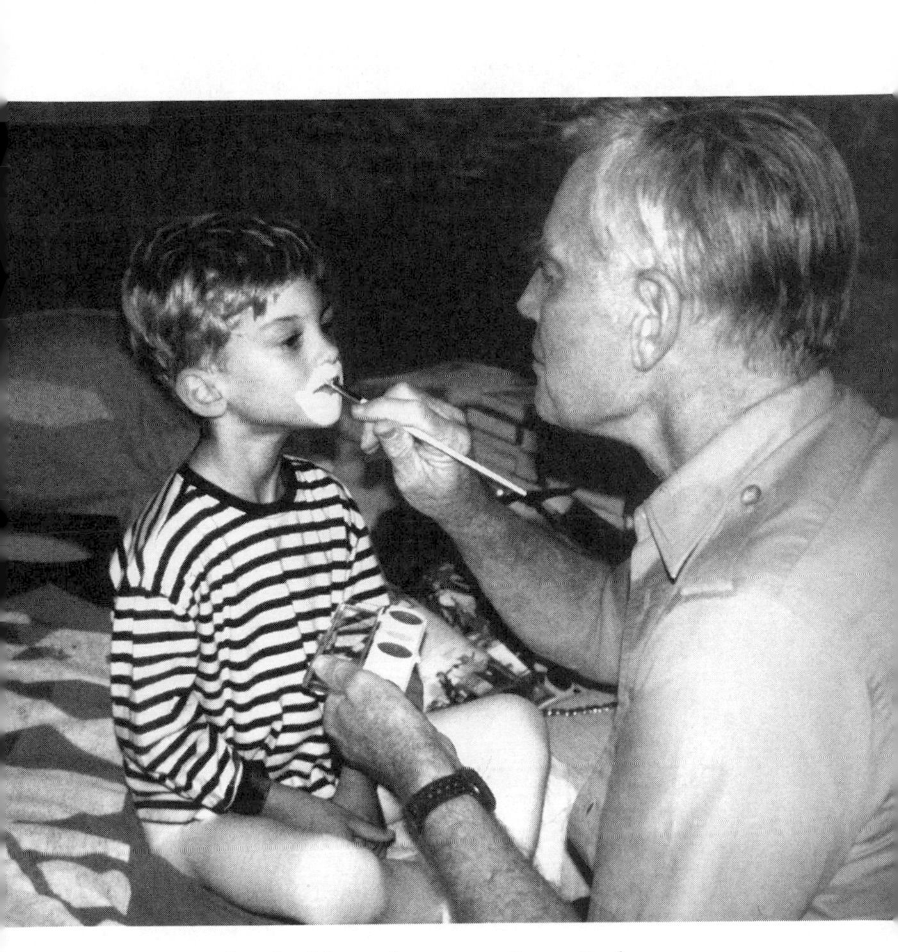

Preparing for the big performance: I gave Jack a professional clown makeup.

Taking a curtain call.

A five-year-old clown, Jack, in the *Big Show* *(Photo courtesy of Marilyn Heston)*

Jack with his "swimming pool" birthday cake, July 25, 1996.

Only last week, your dad called me up on his car phone after dropping you off at school. "I just wanted to tell you," he said, "that your grandson read an entire Dr. Seuss book all the way through, all by himself." You read it to your class that day, too. When I told Nana, she was glad of the time she'd put in with you on phonics. Go, Jack!

A couple of weeks before that, you passed another test, very well. When I picked you up early from school because there were some bad guys robbing a bank and shooting people very close to your school, you seemed very cool when the police talked to me at each intersection.

I'm sure, if things had gone badly and I'd had to say to you, "Jack, lie down on the floor of the car and put that pillow over your head . . . NOW!" you would have done exactly that (remembering to undo your seatbelt).

I know you get some of this discipline from your karate master. That's very good . . . the discipline he's teaching your whole class is admirable . . . also the way all boys seem to understand it.

Still, I think the most fun we had this past month was the school show. Since makeup for a part is something I know how to do, you gave me your face to work with. I made you into a pretty good red-headed, red-nosed clown, didn't I? (The best part of it was your performance, though.)

More and more, Jack, you are growing into being a man. I wish you well in that long, tough journey, still far from over. It's tough to be a man . . . even tougher to be a good one. Still, you've got your teachers, your mom, and Nana to help you, also your dad (who is a *very* good man) to give you good advice. I don't think I need to tell you that you can count on me, even long after you need me. Anytime, anywhere, Jack. Trust me on that. (No, I don't need to tell you that. I know.)

Meantime, just do your best and keep your promises, as you've tried hard always to do. That alone will take you a long way.

I love you,
with all my
heart
Ba

CHAPTER FIVE

Honor

"Honor is a gift a man must give to himself"

— PATRICK HENRY

Honor is, I think, the rarest of all human virtues . . . yet perhaps the most valuable. The higher mammals share some qualities with Man: bravery, some skill at problem solving, protection of the young, and certainly loyalty. Harder to define though, and much harder to possess is honor.

For most of this century, Walt Disney enchanted us with wonderfully engaging anthropomorphic images of a whole galaxy of animal life, from a cricket to a whale. Still, for all their appeal,

Jack and I parading in Walt Disney World. Jack confided to me, "You know Ba, this is the *weal* Mickey Mouse!" He learned the classic wave from a parade car very quickly.

Jack and I at Walt Disney World where we'd both been invited to open the AFI Film Center there. I later gave them the staff I used to part the Red Sea for Mr. DeMille.

(Both photos: © Disney Enterprises, Inc.)

GAP

these are fantasies. Nobody more than ten years old imagines that an animal can perceive, let alone understand, the idea of honor. Men and women in their thousands have died for it . . . for God, for freedom. I hope Jack's put this distinction into something like a real-life perspective . . . even at five.

Patrick Henry knew it in his heart. In the end, honor is a gift that can only be self-bestowed. Each man, in his heart's core, must give it to himself . . . if he dares. A gift only each individual one of us can validate. I flew (rarely) in the Aleutians with another radio gunner named Frank Fielding. He'd earned a Silver Star, flying out of Midway in the battle that was the turning point of World War II.

Talking to me once over several beers, he said "Ah, I was there, that's all. It scared the crap outta me, 'f y'wanna know, but it was the only thing I could *do,* f'God's sake. Now it's this big deal."

I was only faced with an honorable choice once in the war (aside from attending it in the first place, a choice I found unavoidable). Overnight, the atom bomb ended the war, erasing the plan to invade the main islands of Japan from Okinawa, from where we were scheduled to provide air cover, with an estimated casualty list of one million Americans and two million Japanese.

So in March of 1946, instead of dodging kamikazis over Tokyo, I was lying on a bunk in Great Falls, Montana, reading paperbacks, waiting to be discharged from World War II and reunited with my new wife (whom I hadn't seen in more than two years). I was a staff sergeant by then, so they couldn't give me labor assignments while they funnelled through my discharge and travel orders home.

They could, and did, however, give me command of a latrine detail . . . ten men to clean the latrines in the area. Most of the squad were privates and pfcs. One man, though, reported not in fatigues but wearing his Class A uniform. He was older than I (most guys were), bigger than I (most guys weren't), and he had an attitude. (This was rare, in World War II. We all did more or less exactly what they told us).

He was a buck sergeant; as a staff sergeant, I outranked him. However, he also had the Silver Star and the Purple Heart with two clusters, pinned on the left breast of his tunic. "Lemme tell you sumpin', son," he said quietly. "Ah done mah time. Ah showed up f'the war; ah did whut they ast me. Now Ah'm goin' home. Ah be goddamned if Ah scrub shit outta toilets mah las' day in this unifo'm."

I agreed with him. If you win the Silver Star, you should never have to scrub shit for anyone. Still, that didn't address my situation. "Sergeant," I said, "we have a problem. If you don't do what I order you to do, I have to report you. Then they'll bring charges against you, and both of us will be stuck here for at least a month. OK. I now order you to polish the mirrors and put in fresh toilet paper where needed. Can you handle that?"

His eyes glowed for a second, then he chuckled. "Yeah . . . Ah b'lieve Ah can. You pretty slick, son. Thet's awright."

That was the only significant command decision I made in the war. I know it was the right choice and I think it was honorable, but I can't be sure. Honor is an elusive commodity. Ask Patrick Henry.

I have no idea what Mr. Henry would say, facing the chaos that seems increasingly to define our

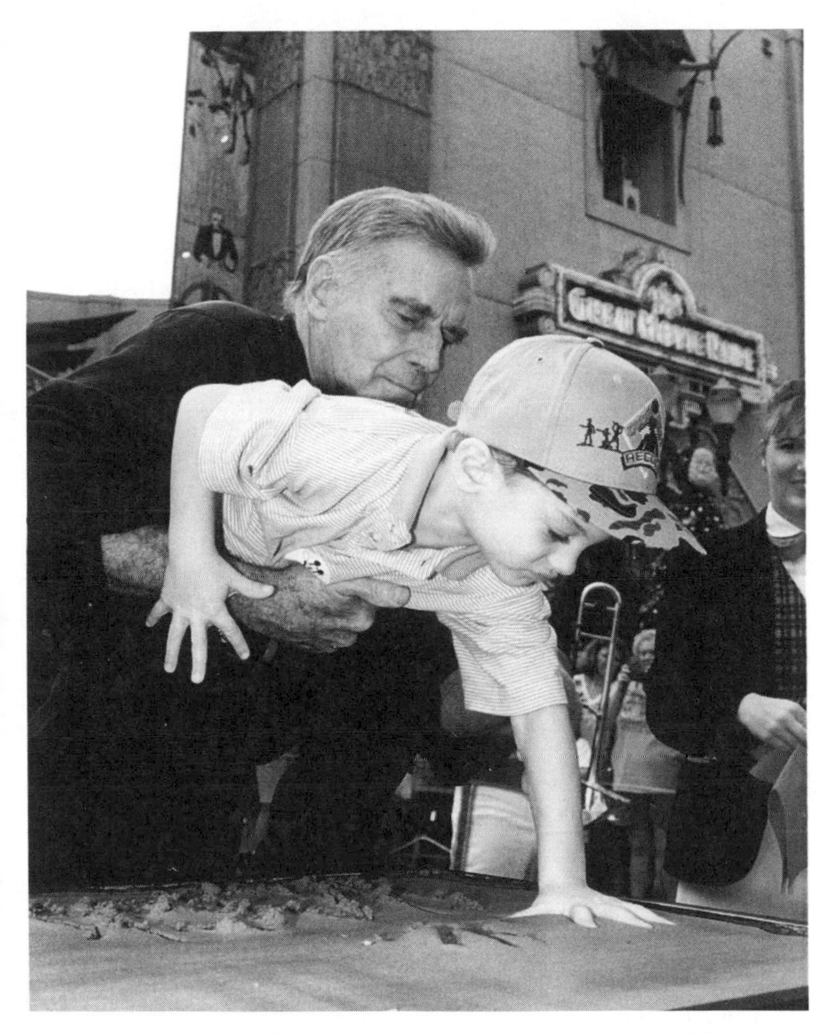

Jack putting his hands in cement at Walt Disney World, not as easy as it looks. *(© Disney Enterprises, Inc.)*

body politic. I know we have to learn to do it better. We try, Lord knows. In this country, we've been trying longer than just about anybody, anywhere else. Still I worry . . . and wonder, when I think about Jack. I hope you understand.

In another twenty years, his generation will be running the whole shebang. Jack, I fervently hope and believe, will by then be doing well whatever he wants and needs to do. What, though!

Making movies, in what by then will be a vastly more enhanced technology (with still, one hopes, some chances for good writing, cutting, and camera work? Yeah, good acting and directing, too, come to think of it?)

Or science, medicine, teaching, something a little more useful to the world. Come to think of it, Jack might someday find happiness in Michigan on the twelve hundred acres and two lakes he'll own there by then, with a good and loving woman and a couple of kids he can teach the wilderness to, as I learned it from my dad, a long time ago, and explored with Jack's dad.

Dear Jack:

This is the end of this book, though a long way from the end of our time together, thank goodness. We have a lot of places to go and things to see yet. I look forward to every one of them.

I've spent a whole day trying to figure out what I should say to you that you haven't already learned about being a good man. A lot of it you already know, from what God said to Moses in the story I read you . . . Don't steal, don't murder, don't lie. The Ten Commandments, they're called. Pretty good rules.

So is the Boy Scout oath. That's a good bunch of guys you may want to join in a few years. They have good rules, too.

But maybe the best set of rules I know on how to be a good man was written by a man whose books you know very well . . . Rudyard Kipling, who wrote *The Jungle Book* and dozens of other wonderful things. Maybe the best thing he wrote, though, is a poem called "If." I believe it says all you need to know about being a man.

If you can keep your head when all about
you
Are losing theirs and blaming it on
you,
If you can trust yourself when all men
doubt you,
But make allowance for their doubting
too;

If you can wait and not be tired by
waiting,
Or being lied about, don't deal in lies,
Or being hated don't give way to hating
And yet don't look too good, nor talk
too wise:

If you can dream—and not make dreams
your master;
If you can think—and not make
thoughts your aim,
If you can meet with Triumph and
Disaster
And treat those two imposters just the
same;
If you can bear to hear the truth you've
spoken
Twisted by knaves to make a trap for
fools,
Or watch the things you gave your life to,
broken,
And stoop and build 'em up with
worn-out tools:

If you can make one heap of all your
winnings;

And risk it on one turn of
pitch-and-toss,
And lose, and start again at your
beginnings
And never breathe a word about your
loss;
If you can force your heart and nerve and
sinew
To serve your turn long after they are
gone,
And so hold on when there is nothing in
you
Except the Will which says to them:
"Hold on!"

If you can talk with crowds and keep
your virtue,
Or walk with kings—nor lose the
common touch,
If neither foes nor loving friends can hurt
you,
If all men count with you, but none
too much;
If you can fill the unforgiving minute
With sixty seconds' worth of distance
run,

Jack helping me to sign my autobiography at Walt Disney World. He even autographed several copies himself, having only recently learned to write his own name. The "Buzz Lightyear" action figure was Jack's favorite trophy from our Disney World adventure. *(© Disney Enterprises, Inc.)*

Yours is the Earth and everything that's
in it,
And—which is more—you'll be a
Man, my son!

All my Love
Ba!